Munschworks

Munschworks

stories by Robert Munsch
illustrations by
Michael Martchenko and Hélène Desputeaux

Annick Press Ltd.
Toronto • New York • Vancouver

Contents

The Paper Bag Princess

by Robert Munsch
illustrated by
Michael Martchenko

Elizabeth was a beautiful princess. She lived in a castle and had expensive princess clothes. She was going to marry a prince named Ronald.

Unfortunately, a dragon smashed her castle, burned all her clothes with his fiery breath, and carried off Prince Ronald.

Elizabeth decided to chase the dragon and get Ronald back.

She looked everywhere for something to wear, but the only thing she could find that was not burnt was a paper bag. So she put on the paper bag and followed the dragon.

He was easy to follow, because he left a trail of burnt forests and horses' bones.

Finally, Elizabeth came to a cave with a large door that had a huge knocker on it. She took hold of the knocker and banged on the door.

The dragon stuck his nose out of the door and said, "Well, a princess! I love to eat princesses, but I have already eaten a whole castle today. I am a very busy dragon. Come back tomorrow."

He slammed the door so fast that Elizabeth almost got her nose caught.

Elizabeth grabbed the knocker and banged on the door again.

The dragon stuck his nose out of the door and said, "Go away. I love to eat princesses, but I have already eaten a whole castle today. I am a very busy dragon. Come back tomorrow."

"Wait," shouted Elizabeth. "Is it true that you are the smartest and fiercest dragon in the whole world?"

"Yes," said the dragon.

"Is it true," said Elizabeth, "that you can burn up ten forests with your fiery breath?"

"Oh, yes," said the dragon, and he took a huge, deep breath and breathed out so much fire that he burnt up fifty forests.

"Fantastic," said Elizabeth, and the dragon took another huge breath and breathed out so much fire that he burnt up one hundred forests.

"Magnificent," said Elizabeth, and the dragon took another huge breath, but this time nothing came out. The dragon didn't even have enough fire left to cook a meatball.

Elizabeth said, "Dragon, is it true that you can fly around the world in just ten seconds?"

"Why, yes," said the dragon, and jumped up and flew all the way around the world in just ten seconds.

He was very tired when he got back, but Elizabeth shouted, "Fantastic, do it again!"

So the dragon jumped up and flew around
the whole world in just twenty seconds.
    When he got back he was too tired to talk,
and he lay down and went straight to sleep.

Elizabeth whispered, very softly, "Hey, dragon." The dragon didn't move at all.

She lifted up the dragon's ear and put her head right inside. She shouted as loud as she could, "Hey, dragon!"

The dragon was so tired he didn't even move.

Elizabeth walked right over the dragon and opened the door to the cave.

There was Prince Ronald. He looked at her and said, "Elizabeth, you are a mess! You smell like ashes, your hair is all tangled and you are wearing a dirty old paper bag. Come back when you are dressed like a real princess."

"Ronald," said Elizabeth, "your clothes are really pretty and your hair is very neat. You look like a real prince, but you are a bum."

They didn't get married after all.

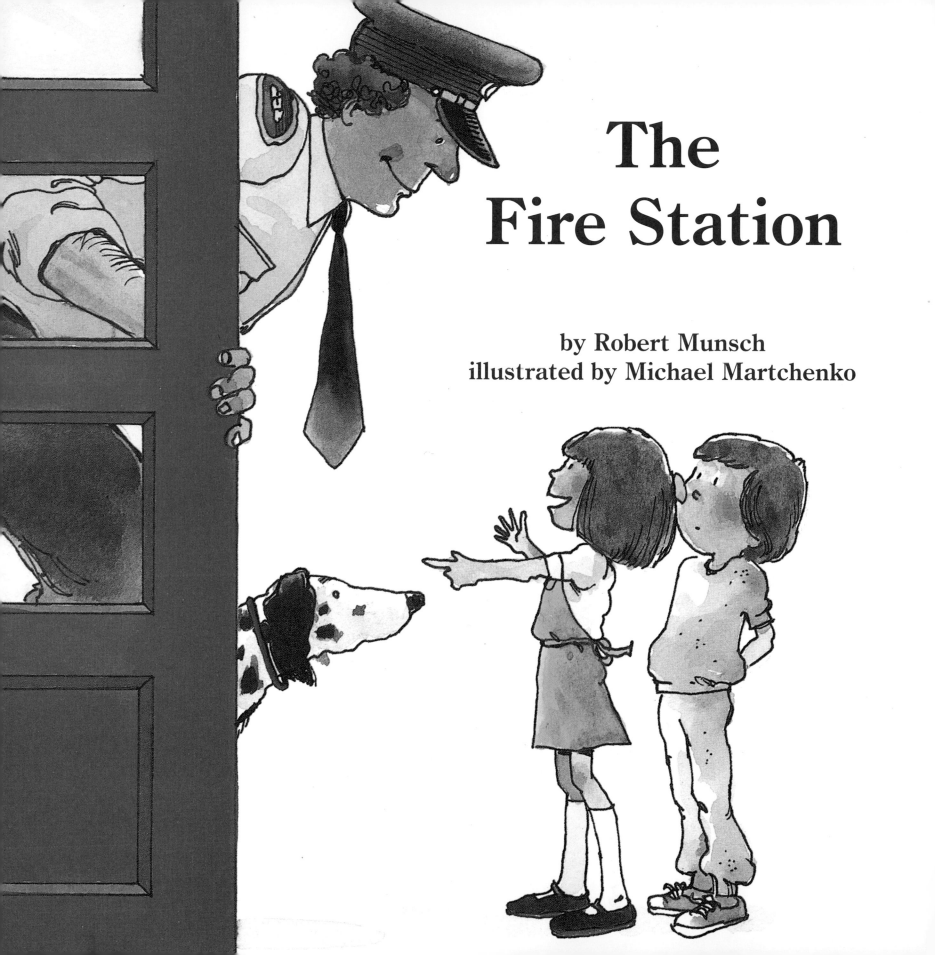

The
Fire Station

by Robert Munsch
illustrated by Michael Martchenko

Michael and Sheila were walking down the street. As they passed the fire station Sheila said, "Michael! Let's go ride a fire truck."

"Well," said Michael, "I think maybe I should ask my mother, and I think maybe I should ask my father and I think maybe..."

"I think we should go in," said Sheila. Then she grabbed Michael's hand and pulled him up to the door.

Sheila knocked: BLAM – BLAM – BLAM – BLAM – BLAM. A large fireman came out and asked, "What can I do for you?"

"Well," said Michael, "maybe you could show us a fire truck and hoses and rubber boots and ladders and all sorts of stuff like that."

"Certainly," said the fireman.

"And maybe," said Sheila, "you will let us drive a fire truck?"

"Certainly not," said the fireman.

They went in and looked at ladders and hoses and big rubber boots. Then they looked at little fire trucks and big fire trucks and enormous fire trucks. When they were done Michael said, "Let's go."

"Right," said Sheila. "Let's go into the enormous fire truck."

While they were in the truck, the fire alarm went off: CLANG – CLANG – CLANG – CLANG – CLANG.

"Oh, no!" said Michael.

"Oh, yes!" said Sheila. Then she grabbed Michael and pulled him into the back seat.

Firemen came running from all over. They slid down poles and ran down stairs. Then they jumped onto the truck and drove off. The firemen didn't look in the back seat. Michael and Sheila were in the back seat.

They came to an enormous fire. Lots of yucky-colored smoke got all over everything. It colored Michael yellow, green and blue. It colored Sheila purple, green and yellow.

When the fire chief saw them he said, "What are you doing here!"

Sheila said, "We came in the fire truck. We thought maybe it was a bus. We thought maybe it was a taxi. We thought maybe it was an elevator. We thought maybe..."

"I think maybe I'd better take you home," said the fire chief. He put Michael and Sheila in his car and drove them away.

When Michael got home he knocked on the door. His mother opened it and said, "You messy boy! You can't come in and play with Michael! You're too dirty." She slammed the door right in Michael's face.

"My own mother," said Michael. "She didn't even know me." He knocked on the door again.

His mother opened the door and said, "You dirty boy! You can't come in and play with Michael. You're too dirty. You're absolutely filthy. You're a total mess. You're...Oh, my!...Oh, no!...YOU'RE MICHAEL!"

Michael went inside and lived in the bathtub for three days until he got clean.

When Sheila came home she knocked on the door. Her father opened it and saw an incredibly messy girl. He said, "You can't come in to play with Sheila. You're too dirty." He slammed the door right in her face.

"Ow," said Sheila. "My own father and he didn't even know me."

She kicked and pounded on the door as loudly as she could. Her father opened the door and said, "Now stop that racket, you dirty girl. You can't come in to play with Sheila. You're too dirty. You're absolutely filthy. You're a total mess. You're...Oh, my!...Oh, no!... YOU'RE SHEILA!"

"Right," said Sheila, "I went to a fire in the back of a fire truck and I got all smoky. I WASN'T EVEN SCARED."

Sheila went inside and lived in the bathtub for five days until she got clean.

Then Michael took Sheila on a walk past the police station. He told her, "If you ever take me in another fire truck, I am going to ask the police to put you in jail."

"JAIL!" yelled Sheila. "Let's go look at the jail! What a great idea!"

"Oh, no!" yelled Michael, and Sheila grabbed his hand and pulled him into the police station.

I Have
to Go!

by Robert Munsch
illustrated by Michael Martchenko

*O*ne day Andrew's mother and father were taking him to see his grandma and grandpa. Before they put him in the car his mother said, "Andrew, do you have to go pee?"

Andrew said, "No, no, no, no, no."

His father said, very slowly and clearly, "Andrew, do you have to go pee?"

"No, no, no, no," said Andrew. "I have decided never to go pee again."

So they put Andrew into the car, fastened his seatbelt and gave him lots of books, and lots of toys, and lots of crayons, and drove off down the road—VAROOMMM. They had been driving for just one minute when Andrew yelled, "I HAVE TO GO PEE!"

"YIKES," said the father.

"OH NO," said the mother.

Then the father said, "Now, Andrew, wait just five minutes. In five minutes we will come to a gas station where you can go pee."

Andrew said, "I have to go pee RIGHT NOW!"

So the mother stopped the car— SCREEEEECH. Andrew jumped out of the car and peed behind a bush.

When they got to Grandma's and Grandpa's house, Andrew wanted to go out to play. It was snowing, and he needed a snowsuit. Before they put on the snowsuit, the mother and the father and the grandma and the grandpa all said, "ANDREW! DO YOU HAVE TO GO PEE?"

Andrew said, "No, no, no, no, no."

So they put on Andrew's snowsuit. It had five zippers, 10 buckles and 17 snaps. It took them half an hour to get the snowsuit on.

Andrew walked out into the back yard, threw one snowball and yelled, "I HAVE TO GO PEE."

The father and the mother and the grandma
and the grandpa all ran outside, got Andrew
out of the snowsuit and carried him to the
bathroom.

When Andrew came back down they had a nice long dinner. Then it was time for Andrew to go to bed.

Before they put Andrew into bed, the mother and the father and the grandma and the grandpa all said, "ANDREW! DO YOU HAVE TO GO PEE?"

Andrew said, "No, no, no, no, no."

So his mother gave him a kiss, and his father gave him a kiss, and his grandma gave him a kiss, and his grandpa gave him a kiss.

"Just wait," said the mother, "he's going to yell and say he has to go pee."

"Oh," said the father, "he does it every night. It's driving me crazy."

The grandmother said, "I never had these problems with my children."

They waited for five minutes, 10 minutes, 15 minutes, 20 minutes.

The father said, "I think he is asleep."

The mother said, "Yes, I think he is asleep."

The grandmother said, "He is definitely asleep and he didn't yell and say he had to go pee."

Then Andrew said, "I wet my bed."

So the mother and the father and the grandma and the grandpa all changed Andrew's bed and Andrew's pajamas. Then the mother gave him a kiss, and the father gave him a kiss, and the grandma gave him a kiss, and the grandpa gave him a kiss, and the grownups all went downstairs.

They waited five minutes, 10 minutes, 15 minutes, 20 minutes, and from upstairs Andrew yelled, "GRANDPA, DO YOU HAVE TO GO PEE?"

And Grandpa said, "Why, yes, I think I do."

Andrew said, "Well, so do I."

So they both went to the bathroom and peed in the toilet, and Andrew did not wet his bed again that night, not even once.

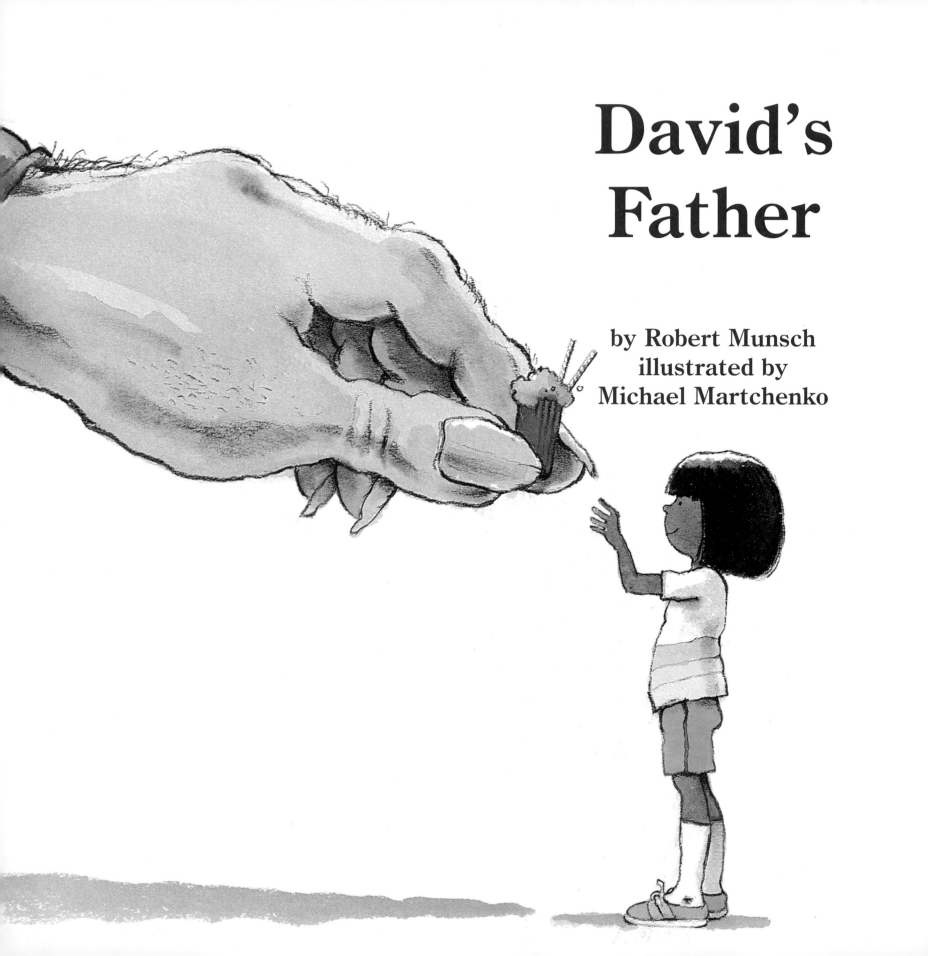

David's Father

by Robert Munsch
illustrated by
Michael Martchenko

Julie was skipping home from school. She came to a large moving van. A man came out carrying a spoon—only it was as big as a shovel. Another man came out carrying a fork—only it was as big as a pitchfork. A third man came out carrying a knife—only it was as big as a flagpole.

"Yikes," said Julie, "I don't want to get to know these people at all."

She ran all the way home and hid under her bed till dinner time.

The next day Julie was skipping home from school again. A boy was standing where the moving van had been. He said, "Hi, my name's David. Would you like to come and play?" Julie looked at him very carefully. He seemed to be a regular sort of boy, so she stayed to play.

At five o'clock, from far away down the street, someone called, "Julie, come and eat."

"That's my mother," said Julie. Then someone called, ***"DAVID!!!"***

"That's my father," said David.

Julie jumped up in the air, ran around in a circle three times, ran home and locked herself in her room till it was time for breakfast the next morning.

The next day Julie was skipping home and she saw David again. He said, "Hi, Julie, do you want to come and play?" Julie looked at him very, very carefully. He seemed to be a regular boy, so she stayed and played.

When it was almost five o'clock, David said, "Julie, please stay for dinner."

But Julie remembered the big knife, the big fork and the big spoon. "Well, I don't know," she said, "maybe it's a bad idea. I think maybe no. Good-bye, good-bye, good-bye."

"Well," said David, "we're having cheeseburgers, chocolate milk shakes and a salad."

"Oh?" said Julie, "I love cheeseburgers. I'll stay, I'll stay."

So they went into the kitchen. There was a small table with cheeseburgers, milk shakes and salads. On the other side of the room there was an enormous table. On it were a spoon as big as a shovel, a fork as big as a pitchfork and a knife as big as a flagpole. "David," whispered Julie, "who sits there?"

"Oh," said David. "That's where my father sits. You can hear him coming now." David's father sounded like this:

broum broum broum

He opened the door.

David's father was a giant. On his table there were 26 snails, three fried octopuses and 16 bricks covered with chocolate sauce.

David and Julie ate their cheeseburgers and the father ate the snails. David and Julie drank their milk shakes and the father ate the fried octopuses. David and Julie ate their salads and the father ate his chocolate-covered bricks.

David's father asked Julie if she would like a
snail. Julie said no. David's father asked Julie if
she would like an octopus. Julie said no.
David's father asked Julie if she would like a
delicious chocolate-covered brick. Julie said,
"No, but please, may I have another milk
shake?" So David's father made her another
milk shake.

When they were done Julie said, very softly so the father couldn't hear, "David, you don't look very much like your father."

"Well, I'm adopted," said David.

"Oh," said Julie. "Well, do you like your father?"

"He's great," said David, "come for a walk and see."

So they walked down the street. Julie and David skipped, and the father went

broum broum broum.

They came to a road and they couldn't get across. The cars would not stop for David. The cars would not stop for Julie. The father walked into the middle of the road, looked at the cars and yelled,

"stop."

The cars all jumped up into the air, ran around in a circle three times and went back up the street so fast they forgot their tires.

Julie and David crossed the street and went into a store. The man who ran the store didn't like serving kids. They waited five minutes, 10 minutes, 15 minutes. Then David's father came in. He looked at the storekeeper and said, ***"THESE KIDS ARE MY FRIENDS!"*** The man jumped up into the air, ran around the store three times and gave David and Julie three boxes of ice cream, 11 bags of potato chips and 19 life savers, all for free. Julie and David walked down the street and went around a bend.

There were six big kids from grade eight standing in the middle of the sidewalk. They looked at David. They looked at Julie and they looked at the food. Then one big kid reached down and grabbed a box of ice cream. David's father came round the bend. He looked at the big kids and yelled,

"beat it."

They jumped right out of their shirts. They jumped right out of their pants and ran down the street in their underwear. Julie ran after them, but she slipped and scraped her elbow.

David's father picked her up and held her.
Then he put a special giant bandage on her elbow.
Julie said, "Well, David, you do have a very
nice father after all, but he is still kind of scary."

"You think he is scary?" said David.
"Wait till you meet my grandmother."

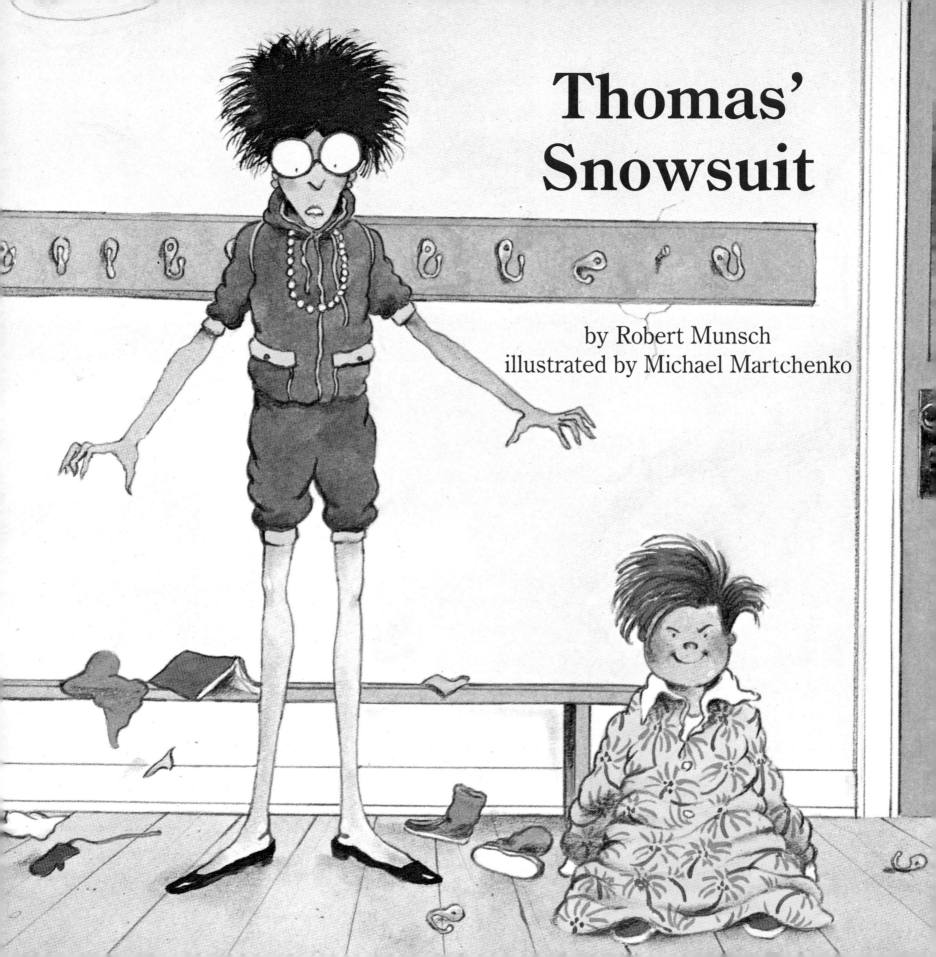

Thomas' Snowsuit

by Robert Munsch
illustrated by Michael Martchenko

One day, Thomas' mother bought him a nice new brown snowsuit. When Thomas saw that snowsuit he said, "That is the ugliest thing I have ever seen in my life. If you think that I am going to wear that ugly snowsuit, you are crazy!"

Thomas' mother said, "We will see about that."

The next day, when it was time to go to school, the mother said, "Thomas, please put on your snowsuit," and Thomas said, "NNNNNO."

His mother jumped up and down and said, "Thomas, put on that snowsuit!"

And Thomas said, "NNNNNO!"

So Thomas' mother picked up Thomas in one hand, picked up the snowsuit in the other hand, and she tried to stick them together. They had an enormous fight, and when it was done Thomas was in his snowsuit.

Thomas went off to school and hung up his snowsuit. When it was time to go outside, all the other kids jumped into their snowsuits and ran out the door. But not Thomas.

The teacher looked at Thomas and said, "Thomas, please put on your snowsuit."

Thomas said, "NNNNNO."

The teacher jumped up and down and said, "Thomas, put on that snowsuit."

And Thomas said, "NNNNNO."

So the teacher picked up Thomas in one hand, picked up the snowsuit in the other hand and she tried to stick them together. They had an enormous fight, and when they were done the teacher was wearing Thomas' snowsuit and Thomas was wearing the teacher's dress.

When the teacher saw what she was wearing, she picked up Thomas in one hand and tried to get him back into his snowsuit. They had an enormous fight. When they were done, the snowsuit and the dress were tied into a great big knot on the floor and Thomas and the teacher were in their underclothes.

Just then the door opened, and in walked the principal. The teacher said, "It's Thomas. He won't put on his snowsuit."

The principal gave his very best
PRINCIPAL LOOK and said, "Thomas, put on
your snowsuit."
And Thomas said, "NNNNNO."

So the principal picked up Thomas in one hand and he picked up the teacher in the other hand, and he tried to get them back into their clothes. When he was done, the principal was wearing the teacher's dress, the teacher was wearing the principal's suit and Thomas was still in his underwear.

Then from far out in the playground some-one yelled, "Thomas, come and play!" Thomas ran across the room, jumped into his snowsuit, got his boots on in two seconds and ran out the door.

The principal looked at the teacher and said, "Hey, you have on my suit. Take it off right now."

The teacher said, "Oh, no. You have on my dress. You take off my dress first."

Well, they argued and argued and argued, but neither one wanted to change first.

Finally, Thomas came in from recess. He looked at the principal and he looked at the teacher. Thomas picked up the principal in one hand. He picked up the teacher in the other hand. They had an enormous fight and Thomas got everybody back into their clothes.

The next day the principal quit his job and
moved to Arizona, where nobody ever wears a
snowsuit.

Pigs

by Robert Munsch
illustrated by
Michael Martchenko

*M*egan's father asked her to feed the pigs on her way to school. He said, "Megan, please feed the pigs, but don't open the gate. Pigs are smarter than you think. Don't open the gate."

"Right," said Megan. "I will not open the gate. Not me. No sir. No, no, no, no, no."

So Megan went to the pig pen. She looked at the pigs. The pigs looked at Megan.

Megan said, "These are the dumbest-looking animals I have ever seen. They stand there like lumps on a bump. They wouldn't do anything if I did open the gate." So Megan opened the gate just a little bit. The pigs stood there and looked at Megan. They didn't do anything.

Megan said, "These are the dumbest-looking animals I have ever seen. They stand there like lumps on a bump. They wouldn't even go out the door if the house was on fire." So Megan opened the gate a little bit more. The pigs stood there and looked at Megan. They didn't do anything.

Then Megan yelled, "HEY YOU DUMB PIGS!" The pigs jumped up and ran right over Megan, WAP—WAP—WAP—WAP —WAP, and out the gate.

When Megan got up she couldn't see the pigs anywhere. She said, "Uh-oh, I am in bad trouble. Maybe pigs are not so dumb after all." Then she went to tell her father the bad news. When she got to the house Megan heard a noise coming from the kitchen. It went, "OINK, OINK, OINK."

"That doesn't sound like my mother. That doesn't sound like my father. That sounds like pigs."

She looked in the window. There was her father, sitting at the breakfast table. A pig was drinking his coffee. A pig was eating his newspaper. And a pig was peeing on his shoe.

"Megan," yelled her father, "you opened the gate. Get these pigs out of here."

Megan opened the front door a little bit. The pigs stood and looked at Megan. Finally Megan opened the front door all the way and yelled, "HEY YOU DUMB PIGS!" The pigs jumped up and ran right over Megan, WAP—WAP—WAP—WAP—WAP, and out the door.

Megan ran outside, chased all the pigs into the pig pen and shut the gate. Then she looked at the pigs and said, "You are still dumb, like lumps on a bump." Then she ran off to school. Just as she was about to open the front door, she heard a sound: "OINK, OINK, OINK."

She said, "That doesn't sound like my
teacher. That doesn't sound like the principal.
That sounds like pigs."

Megan looked in the principal's window.
There was a pig drinking the principal's coffee.
A pig was eating the principal's newspaper.
And a pig was peeing on the principal's shoe.
The principal yelled, "Megan, get these pigs
out of here!"

Megan opened the front door of the school a little bit. The pigs didn't do anything. She opened the door a little bit more. The pigs still didn't do anything. She opened the door all the way and yelled, "HEY YOU DUMB PIGS!" The pigs jumped up and ran right over Megan, WAP—WAP—WAP—WAP—WAP, and out the door.

Megan went into the school. She sat down at her desk and said, "That's that! I finally got rid of all the pigs." Then she heard a noise: "OINK, OINK, OINK." Megan opened her desk, and there was a new baby pig. The teacher said, "Megan! Get that dumb pig out of here!"

Megan said, "Dumb? Who ever said pigs were dumb? Pigs are smart. I am going to keep it for a pet."

At the end of the day the school bus finally came. Megan walked up to the door, then heard something say, "OINK, OINK, OINK."

Megan said, "That doesn't sound like the bus driver. That sounds like a pig." She climbed up the stairs and looked in the bus. There was a pig driving the bus, pigs eating the seats and pigs lying in the aisle.

A pig shut the door and drove the bus down the road.

It drove the bus all the way to Megan's farm, through the barnyard and right into the pig pen.

Megan got out of the bus, walked across the barnyard and marched into the kitchen. She said, "The pigs are all back in the pig pen. They came back by themselves. Pigs are smarter than you think."

And Megan never let out any more animals.

At least, not any more pigs.

Mortimer

by Robert Munsch
illustrated by
Michael Martchenko

One night Mortimer's mother took him upstairs to go to bed—

thump
thump
thump
thump
thump
thump.

When they got upstairs Mortimer's mother opened the door to his room.

She threw him into bed and said,

"MORTIMER, BE QUIET."

Mortimer shook his head, yes.

The mother shut the door.
Then she went back down the stairs—
thump
  thump
    thump
      thump
        thump.

As soon as she got back downstairs
Mortimer sang,

    Clang, clang, rattle-bing-bang
    Gonna make my noise all day.
    Clang, clang, rattle-bing-bang
    Gonna make my noise all day.

Mortimer's father heard all that noise. He came up the stairs—

thump thump thump thump thump thump.

He opened the door and yelled,

"MORTIMER, BE QUIET."

Mortimer shook his head, yes.

The father went back down the stairs—
thump thump thump thump thump.

As soon as he got to the bottom of the
stairs Mortimer sang,

    Clang, clang, rattle-bing-bang
    Gonna make my noise all day.
    Clang, clang, rattle-bing-bang
    Gonna make my noise all day.

All of Mortimer's seventeen brothers and sisters heard that noise, and they all came up the stairs—

thump thump thump thump thump thump

They opened the door and yelled in a tremendous, loud voice,

"MORTIMER, BE QUIET."

Mortimer shook his head, yes.

The brothers and sisters shut the door
and went downstairs—
thump
   thump
      thump
         thump
            thump.

As soon as they got to the bottom of the
stairs Mortimer sang,

Clang, clang, rattle-bing-bang
Gonna make my noise all day.
Clang, clang, rattle-bing-bang
Gonna make my noise all day.

They got so upset that they called the police. Two policemen came and they walked very slowly up the stairs—

thump thump thump thump thump thump.

They opened the door and said in very deep, policemen-type voices,

"MORTIMER, BE QUIET."

The policemen shut the door and went
back down the stairs—
thump
  thump
    thump
      thump
        thump.

As soon as they got to the bottom of the
stairs Mortimer sang,

> Clang, clang, rattle-bing-bang
> Gonna make my noise all day.
> Clang, clang, rattle-bing-bang
> Gonna make my noise all day.

Well, downstairs no one knew what to do.
The mother got into a big fight with the policemen.
The father got into a big fight with the brothers and sisters.

Upstairs, Mortimer got so tired waiting for someone to come up that he fell asleep.

Purple, Green and Yellow

by Robert Munsch
illustrated by
Hélène Desputeaux

*B*rigid went to her mother and said, "I need some coloring markers. All my friends have coloring markers. They draw wonderful pictures. Mommy, I need some coloring markers."

"Oh, no!" said her mother. "I've heard about those coloring markers. Kids draw on walls, they draw on the floor, they draw on themselves. You can't have any coloring markers."

"Well," said Brigid, "there are these new coloring markers. They wash off with just water. I can't get into any trouble with coloring markers that wash off. Get me some of those."

"Well," said her mother, "all right."

So her mother went out and got Brigid 500 washable coloring markers.

Brigid went up to her room and drew wonderful pictures. She drew lemons that were yellower than lemons, and roses that were redder than roses, and oranges that were oranger than oranges.

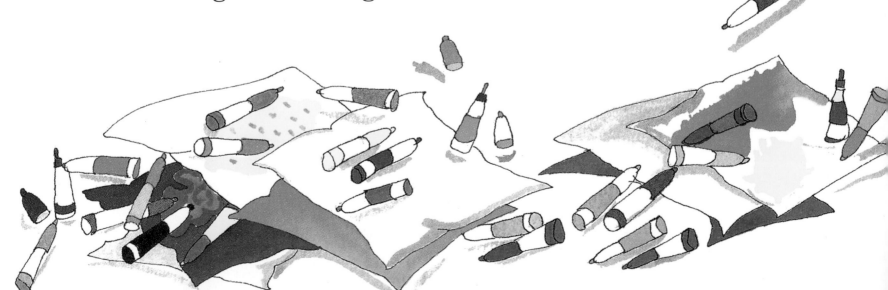

Her mother was amazed. She said,
"Wow! My kid is an artist."

But after a week Brigid got bored. She went to her mother and said, "Mom, did I draw on the wall?"

"Nnnnooo," said her mother. "Did I draw on the floor?"

"Nnnnooo," said her mother. "Did I draw on myself?"

"Nnnnooo," said her mother.

"Well," said Brigid, "I didn't get into any trouble and I need some new coloring markers. All my friends have them. Mommy, there are coloring markers that smell. They have ones that smell like roses and lemons and oranges and even ones that smell like cow plops. Mom, they have coloring markers that smell like anything you want! Mom, I need those coloring markers."

Her mother went out and got 500 coloring markers that smelled. Then Brigid went upstairs and she drew pictures. She drew lemons that smelled like lemons, and roses that smelled like roses, and oranges that smelled like oranges, and cow plops that smelled like cow plops.

Her mother said, "Wow! My kid is an artist."

184

But after a week Brigid got bored. She said, "Mom, did I draw on the floor?"

"Nnnnooo," said her mother.

"Did I draw on the walls?"

"Nnnnooo," said her mother.

"Did I draw on myself?"

"Nnnnooo," said her mother.

"Well," said Brigid, "I need some new coloring markers. These are the best kind. All my friends have them. They are super-indelible-never-come-off-till-you're-dead-and-maybe-even-later coloring markers. Mom, I need them."

So her mother went out and got 500 super-indelible-never-come-off-till-you're-dead-and-maybe-even-later coloring markers. Brigid took them and drew pictures for three weeks. She drew lemons that looked better than lemons, and roses that looked better than roses and oranges that looked better than oranges and sunsets that looked better than sunsets.

Then she got bored.

She said, "I'm tired of drawing on the paper. But I am not going to draw on the walls and I am not going to draw on the floor and I'm not going to draw on myself —but everybody knows it's okay to color your finger-nails. Even my mother colors her fingernails."

So Brigid took a purple super-indelible-never-come-off-till-you're-dead-and-maybe-even-later coloring marker, and she colored her thumbnail bright purple.

And that was so pretty, she colored all her fingernails purple, black and yellow.

And that was so pretty, she colored her hands yellow, green and red.

189

And that was so pretty, she colored her face purple, green, yellow and blue.

And that was so pretty, she colored her belly-button blue.

And that was so pretty, she colored herself all sorts of colors almost entirely all over.

Then Brigid looked in the mirror and said, "What have I done! My mother is going to kill me." So she ran into the bathroom and washed her hands for half an hour. Nothing came off. Her hands still looked like mixed-up rainbows.

Then she had a wonderful idea.

She reached way down into the bottom of the coloring markers and got a special-colored marker. It was the same color she was. She took that marker and colored herself all over until she was her regular color again. In fact, she looked even better than before—almost too good to be true.

She went downstairs and her mother said, "Why, Brigid, you're looking really good today."

"Right," said Brigid.

Then her mother said, "It's time to wash your hands for dinner."

But Brigid was afraid that the special color would not stick to the colors underneath, so she said, "I already washed my hands."

But her mother smelled her hands and said, "Ahhh. No soap!" She took Brigid into the bathroom and washed her hands and face. All the special color came off and Brigid looked like mixed-up rainbows.

"Oh, no!" said her mother. "Brigid, did you color your hands with the coloring markers that wash off?"

"Nnnnooo."

"Brigid, did you color your hands with the coloring markers that smell?"

"Nnnnnooooo."

"Did you use the super-indelible-never-come-off-till-you're-dead-and-maybe-even-later coloring markers?"

"Yes!"

"Yikes!" yelled her mother.

She called the doctor and said, "HELP! HELP! HELP! My daughter has colored herself with super-indelible-never-come-off-till-you're-dead-and-maybe-even-later coloring markers."

"Oh, dear," said the doctor. "Sometimes they never come off."

The doctor came over and gave Brigid a large, orange pill. She said, "Take this pill, wait five minutes and then take a bath."

So Brigid took the pill, waited five minutes, and jumped into the bathtub. Her mother stood outside the door and yelled, "Is it working? Is it working?"

"Yes," said Brigid. "Everything is coming off." And Brigid was right, everything had come off. When Brigid walked out of the bathroom she was invisible.

"Oh, no," yelled her mother. "You can't go to school if you're invisible. You can't go to university if you're invisible. You'll never get a job if you're invisible. Brigid, you've wrecked your life!"

"Don't worry," said Brigid. She ran into her room, got the special-colored marker and colored herself entirely all over until you couldn't tell the difference. In fact, she looked even better than before — almost too good to be true.

But her mother said, "Brigid, you can't go through life like that. You're just a picture. Everyone will know there is something wrong."

"No they won't," said Brigid.

"Yes they will," said her mother.

"No they won't," said Brigid. "I colored Daddy while he was taking a nap and you haven't noticed anything yet!"

"Good heavens!" yelled her mother, and she ran into the living-room and looked at Daddy. He looked even better than before—almost too good to be true.

"Doesn't he look great?" asked Brigid.

"I couldn't even tell the difference," said her mother.

"Right," said Brigid, "and neither will he...

As long as he doesn't get wet."

Murmel, Murmel, Murmel

by Robert Munsch
illustrated by
Michael Martchenko

When Robin went out into her back yard, there was a large hole right in the middle of her sandbox. She knelt down beside it and yelled, "ANYBODY DOWN THERE?"

From way down the hole something said, "Murmel, murmel, murmel."

"Hmmm," said Robin, "very strange." So she yelled, even louder, "ANYBODY DOWN THERE?"

"Murmel, murmel, murmel," said the hole. Robin reached down the hole as far as she could and gave an enormous yank. Out popped a baby.

"Murmel, murmel, murmel," said the baby.

"Murmel, yourself," said Robin. "I am only five years old and I can't take care of a baby. I will find somebody else to take care of you."

Robin picked up the very heavy baby and walked down the street. She met a woman pushing a baby carriage. Robin said, "Excuse me, do you need a baby?"

"Heavens, no," said the woman. "I already have a baby." She went off down the street and seventeen diaper salesmen jumped out from behind a hedge and ran after her.

Robin picked up the baby and went on down the street. She met an old woman and said, "Excuse me, do you need a baby?"

"Does it pee its pants?" said the old lady.

"Yes," said Robin.

"Yecch," said the old lady. "Does it dirty its diaper?"

"Yes," said Robin.

"Yecch," said the old lady. "Does it have a runny nose?"

"Yes," said Robin.

"Yecch," said the old lady. "I already have seventeen cats. I don't need a baby." She went off down the street. Seventeen cats jumped out of a garbage can and ran after her.

Robin picked up the baby and went down the street. She met a woman in fancy clothes. "Excuse me," said Robin, "do you need a baby?"

"Heavens, no," said the woman. "I have seventeen jobs, lots of money and no time. I don't need a baby." She went off down the street. Seventeen secretaries, nine messengers and a pizza delivery man ran after her.

"Rats," said Robin. She picked up the baby and walked down the street. She met a man. "Excuse me," she said, "do you need a baby?"

"I don't know," said the man. "Can it wash my car?"

"No," said Robin.

"Can I sell it for lots of money?"

"No," said Robin.

"Well, what is it for?" said the man.

"It is for loving and hugging and feeding and burping," said Robin.

"I certainly don't need that," said the man. He went off down the street. Nobody followed him.

Robin sat down beside the street, for the baby was getting very heavy.

"Murmel, murmel, murmel," said the baby.

"Murmel, yourself," said Robin. "What am I going to do with you?"

An enormous truck came by and stopped.

A truck driver jumped out and walked around Robin three times. Then he looked at the baby.

"Excuse me," said Robin, "do you need a baby?"

The truck driver said, "Weeeellll..."

"Murmel, murmel, murmel," said the baby.

"Did you say, 'murmel, murmel, murmel'?"asked the truck driver.

"Yes!" said the baby.

"I need you," yelled the truck driver. He picked up the baby and started walking down the street.

"Wait," said Robin, "you forgot your truck!"

"I already have seventeen trucks," said the truck driver. "What I need is a baby..."

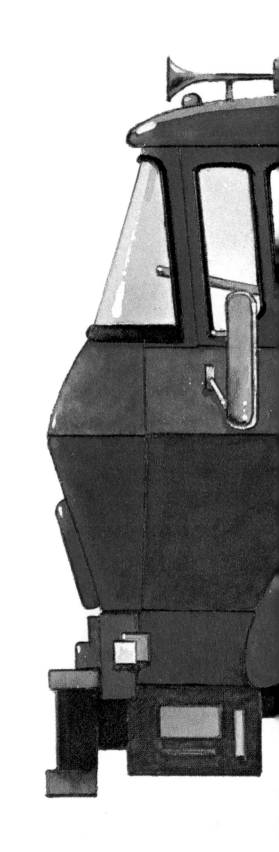

Something Good

by Robert Munsch
illustrated by
Michael Martchenko

*T*yya went shopping with her father and her brother and her sister. She pushed the cart up the aisle and down the aisle, up the aisle and down the aisle, up the aisle and down the aisle.

Tyya said, "Sometimes my father doesn't buy good food. He gets bread, eggs, milk, cheese, spinach—nothing any good! He doesn't buy ICE CREAM! COOKIES! CHOCOLATE BARS! or GINGER ALE!"

So Tyya very quietly snuck away from her father and got a cart of her own. She pushed it over to the ice cream. Then she put one hundred boxes of ice cream into her cart.

Tyya pushed that cart up behind her father and said, "DADDY, LOOK!" Her father turned around and yelled, "YIKES!"

Tyya said, "DADDY! GOOD FOOD!"

"Oh, no," said her father. "This is sugary junk. It will rot your teeth. It will lower your IQ. Put it ALL BACK!"

So Tyya put back the one hundred boxes of ice cream. She meant to go right back to her father, but on the way she had to pass the candy. She put three hundred chocolate bars into her cart.

Tyya pushed that cart up behind her father and said, "DADDY, LOOK!" Her father turned around and said, "YIKES!"

Tyya said, "DADDY! GOOD FOOD!"

"Oh, no," said her father. "This is sugary junk. Put it ALL BACK!" So Tyya put back all the chocolate bars. Then her father said, "Okay, Tyya, I have had it. You stand here and DON'T MOVE."

Tyya knew she was in BIG trouble, so she stood there and DIDN'T MOVE. Some friends came by and said hello. Tyya didn't move. A man ran over her toe with his cart. Tyya still didn't move.

A lady who worked at the store came by and looked at Tyya. She looked her over from the top down, and she looked her over from the bottom up. She knocked Tyya on the head—and Tyya still didn't move.

The lady said, "This is the nicest doll I have ever seen. It looks almost real." She put a price tag on Tyya's nose that said $29.95. Then she picked Tyya up and put her on the shelf with all the other dolls.

A man came along and looked at Tyya. He said, "This is the nicest doll I have ever seen. I'm going to get that doll for my son." He picked up Tyya by the hair.

Tyya yelled, very loudly, "STOP."

The man screamed, "EYAAAAH! IT'S ALIVE!" And he ran down the aisle, knocking over a pile of five hundred apples.

A lady came along and looked at Tyya. She said, "This is the nicest doll I have ever seen. I think I will buy this doll for my daughter." She picked up Tyya by the ear. Tyya yelled, as loudly as she could, "STOP."

The lady screamed, "EYAAAAH! IT'S ALIVE!" And she ran down the aisle, knocking over a pile of five hundred oranges.

Then Tyya's father came along, looking for his daughter. He said, "Tyya? Tyya? Tyya? Tyya? Where are you? ... TYYA! What are you doing on that shelf?"

Tyya said, "It's all your fault. You told me not to move and people are trying to buy me, WAAAAAHHHHH!"

"Oh, come now," said her father. "I won't let anybody buy you." He gave Tyya a big kiss and a big hug; then they went to pay for all the food.

The man at the cash register looked at Tyya and said, "Hey, Mister, you can't take that kid out of the store. You have to pay for her. It says so right on her nose: twenty-nine ninety-five."

"Wait," said the father. "This is my own kid. I don't have to pay for my own kid."

The man said, "If it has a price tag, you have to pay for it."

"I won't pay," said the father.

"You've got to," said the man.

The father said, "NNNNO."

The man said, "YYYYES."

The father said, "NNNNO!"

The man said, "YYYYES!"

The father and Andrew and Julie all yelled, "NNNNNNO!"

Then Tyya quietly said, "Daddy, don't you think I'm worth twenty-nine ninety-five?"

"Ah...Um...I mean... Well, of course you're worth twenty-nine ninety-five," said the father. He reached into his wallet, got out the money, paid the man, and took the price tag off Tyya's nose.

Tyya gave her father a big kiss, SMMMER-CCHH, and a big hug, MMMMMMMMMM, and then she said, "Daddy, you finally bought something good after all."

Then her father picked up Tyya and gave her a big long hug—and didn't say anything at all.

The Munsch for Kids series:

The Dark
Mud Puddle
The Paper Bag Princess
The Boy in the Drawer
Jonathan Cleaned Up—Then He Heard a Sound
Murmel, Murmel, Murmel
Millicent and the Wind
Mortimer
The Fire Station
Angela's Airplane
David's Father
Thomas' Snowsuit
50 Below Zero
I Have to Go!
Moira's Birthday
A Promise is a Promise
Pigs
Something Good
Show and Tell
Purple, Green and Yellow
Wait and See
Where is Gah-Ning?
From Far Away
Stephanie's Ponytail

———————————

Munschworks: The First Munsch Collection
Munschworks 2: The Second Munsch Treasury
Munschworks 3: The Third Munsch Treasury

———————————

Many Munsch titles are available in French and/or
Spanish. Please contact your favorite supplier.